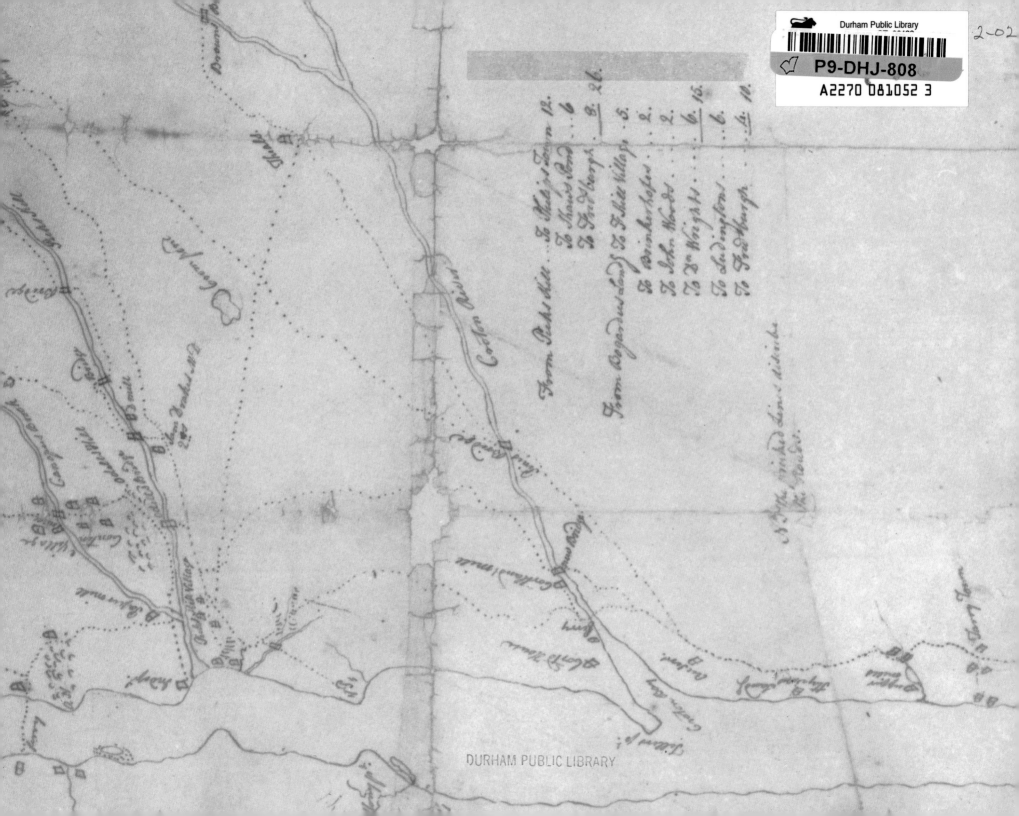

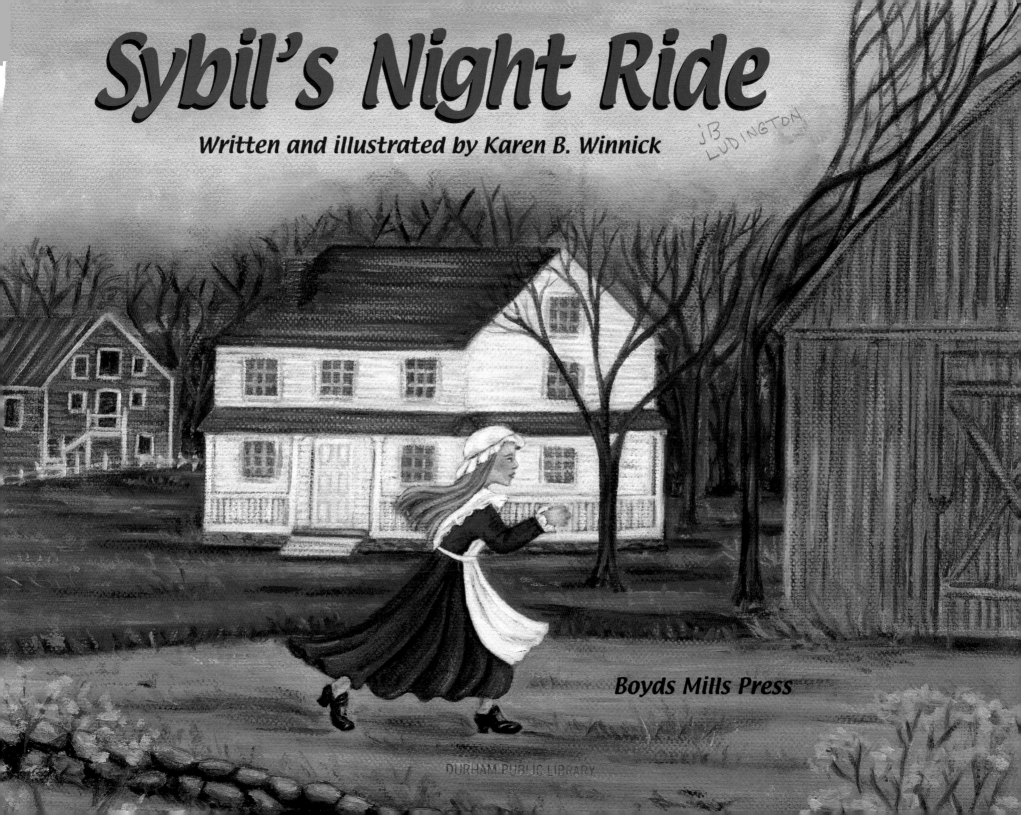

Sybil's Night Ride

Written and illustrated by Karen B. Winnick

Boyds Mills Press

For my father, Sandy Binkoff
with special thanks to Hilary Breed and Richard Muscarella

Author's Note

Sybil Ludington was a Revolutionary War heroine. She was born April 5, 1761, and grew up on a farm in what was Fredricksburg, part of southern Dutchess County in New York. Today this area is in Putnam County.

Sybil's father, Colonel Henry Ludington, was an aide-de-camp to General Washington during the Battle of White Plains.

On April 26, 1777, when this story takes place, Colonel Ludington had just arrived home from gathering supplies for his militia. After Sybil sounded the alert, her father's regiment marched to turn back the British. Ludington's men were too late to save the town of Danbury, but they joined forces with the regiments of General Wooster, General Silliman, and General Benedict Arnold (later a traitor) to attack the Redcoats. The four regiments pushed the British south to Ridgefield, then down to Long Island Sound, where they fled by boat back to New York City.

If you follow Sybil's journey now, you can see historic markers all along the way. There is even a statue of Sybil and her horse Star on the route in Carmel, New York.

Sybil rode forty miles alone on a rainy night. Two hundred and twenty years to the day, I followed her trail in a car on a sunny day. What great admiration I have for this brave young girl!

Karen B. Winnick

Publisher Cataloging-in-Publication Data
Winnick, Karen B.
   Sybil's Night Ride / by Karen B. Winnick. 1st ed. [32]p. : col. ill. ; cm.
Summary: The true story of the young Sybil Ludington, who, like Paul Revere, rode through the countryside to alert the colonists that the British were coming.
ISBN 1-56397-697-8

1. Ludington, Sybil, b. 1761--Juvenile
literature. 2. Danbury (Conn.)--History--Burning by the British, 1777--Juvenile literature.
3. United States--History--Revolution, 1775-1783--Biography--Juvenile literature.
4. United States--History--Revolution, 1775-1783--Women--Juvenile literature.
[1. Ludington, Sybil, b. 1761. 2. Danbury (Conn.)--History--Burning by the British, 1777. 3. United States--History--Revolution, 1775-1783--Biography.
4. Women--Biography.] I. Title.
973.3 / 33 -dc21 2000   AC CIP
99-62643

Text and illustrations copyright © 2000 by Karen B. Winnick
Endpaper map reproduced through the courtesy of the William L. Clements Library, University of Michigan.

Published by Caroline House
Boyds Mills Press, Inc.
A Highlights Company
815 Church Street
Honesdale, Pennsylvania 18431
Printed in China

First edition, 2000
The text of this book is set in Usherwood Bold.

Visit our website:
www.boydsmillspress.com

10 9 8 7 6 5 4 3 2

Sybil slipped out to the barn to check on the colt, Star.
Overhead, low dark clouds were gathering.

She stroked Star's neck and mane. "Imagine," she said,
"Father has been gone all these weeks in search of supplies for his
militia. Tonight he will finally be home! Wait until he sees how
well I have trained you."

Back by the kitchen hearth, Sybil helped her mother
set down the pewter plates for dinner. As Sybil lit the candles,
there was the sound of hoof beats.

She ran down the porch steps. Large drops of rain were
falling. "Father!" she shouted. "Father is home!"

Her mother and younger brothers and sisters rushed out
to greet him.

All through supper, heavy rain pelted the roof and window-panes. Father told about the supplies of medicine, clothing, and gunpowder he had secured for his militia. Everyone asked questions.

"Was it dangerous?"

"Are there enough guns?"

"Are the supplies well hidden?"

Father was explaining that more hiding places needed to be found when, suddenly, someone pounded on the door.

Sybil turned to the mantle clock. It was past nine. Who could it be?

A young man, drenched with rain and mud, stood on the porch.
"Colonel Ludington! The British are burning Danbury."
He stopped to catch his breath. "Look!" He pointed east.
A huge red fireball glowed in the sky.

"The storehouse!" Father cried. "Our supplies!"

"The Redcoats are marching this way," warned the messenger. "They must be turned back!"

"I have four hundred men throughout the county," said Father. "It is urgent they are called to muster."

The messenger shook his head. "My horse and I can ride no farther this night."

Father frowned. "I must remain here to ready the men to march."

Sybil listened closely. Someone was needed to call out the Patriots. She would be brave, brave like Father.

She stepped forward. "I can go, Father. I can ride the colt. For the whole month you were gone, I rode Star every day."

"It is too dangerous," Father said. "The men are scattered far from one another."

"But I know the way," insisted Sybil. "I know the farms of our Patriots."

"There could be spies along the way," said Mother, "or worse, thieves and skinners."

Father shook his head. "This is no night for a young girl to ride alone."

"But there is no one else," Sybil touched Father's arm. "Please, let me go."

Father looked out the window at the fiery red sky. Then he turned and looked at his wife. He sighed. "Sybil, hurry and dress in warm clothing," he said. "Mother and I will wait for you in the barn."

Sybil pulled on her father's old breeches and tucked them into her boots. She threw on her cloak and hat and dashed through puddles to the barn.

Father slid a blanket and saddle onto Star's back. Sybil tightened the cinch. She put on the bridle, threw back the hemp reins, and jumped on.

"Be careful," said Mother, tucking a small pouch of bread and cheese inside Sybil's cloak.

Father squeezed her hand. "First head east, then south, and stay to the roads. When you get to the farm of a Patriot, alert him and ride on quickly. God be with you, my daughter."

Sybil slapped Star's flank. He took off at a gallop past Father's gristmill. He crossed the rain-soaked fields. Mud splashed up over Sybil's boots, sopping her legs. She pressed Star towards the narrow trail between the birches and kept her head low.

Water poured down from the night sky. It dripped off the brim of Sybil's hat and drenched her cloak. She shivered.

Rain and darkness blurred the trail. Sybil rode for a long time over patches of slippery leaves. "Careful, Star," she said. But Star seemed to veer by instinct along the narrow turns.

Strands of wet hair stuck to Sybil's face. She pushed them back and wiped the cold rain from her cheeks.

A roaring sound came through the trees. Star's ears pricked up. "It's only the Mill Stream," Sybil said gently.

They traveled the path south along the rain-swollen stream.
Star stepped through deep mud. His hooves made slushing noises.
Sybil urged him on. She thought how much Father was counting on
her. Would she and Star make it?

She swallowed the lump in her throat, then shouted, "Faster,
Star, *faster*."

A loud rustling came from the trees. Star jerked back. Sybil gripped the reins. "Steady, boy." A deer suddenly leaped out and crossed their path.

On and on they went. Following the curve of the stream, they headed west.

Finally, they neared a farmhouse. "It belongs to one of Father's men," said Sybil. She broke off a branch of a tree. Swiftly, she rode up and banged the branch on the door.

"Muster at Ludington's!" she shouted.

The glow from a candle shone in a window. The door opened, and a man came out.

"Muster at Ludington's!" Sybil cried. "The British are burning Danbury!"

The man waved, and Sybil rode on.

She turned Star onto the path heading north, uphill through dense woods. The wind whistled eerily. Sky and trees together were black as coal. Sybil knew it would be easy to lose her way. And thieves could be lurking.

Holding tight, she leaned close to Star's back. "We can do it, Star."

Climbing, Star panted as he made his way through the wet,
thick brush. Twigs split and snapped, scratching Sybil's arms. Once,
Star stumbled on a rock. Sybil slid from the saddle to check his leg.
It seemed like forever before they began to travel down the slope.

At the bottom of the hill, a clearing appeared. Several farmhouses were set behind a wooden fence.

"Finally!" Taking a deep breath, Sybil gripped her branch. She rode up to the closest house and banged on the door. "Muster at Ludington's!"

She rapped on one door after another. "The British are burning Danbury!" She pointed east. "See the red sky!"

Dogs barked. Horses whinnied. One by one, candles were lit. Doors opened. People holding lanterns peered out.

"Turn back the Redcoats!" Sybil cried. "Muster at Ludington's!"

Farther down the road, she banged on the door of the blacksmith's house. She rode up to the cooper's house, and then to the tanner's.

"Muster at Ludington's!" she shouted again and again.

Men ran out. They grabbed their muskets and saddled their horses.

Sybil rode on past the cemetery, along the edge of the lake rippling with rain. Ahead, pastures stretched out, separated by low stone walls. More and more houses appeared.

Over and over Sybil cried out to the Patriots: "Hurry, come muster! Go to Ludington's! Turn back the Redcoats!"

Close to the road stood a barn. The door abruptly opened, and a man carrying a lantern and a pail walked out.

Sybil shuddered. It was a loyalist farmer Father suspected of being a British spy.

She slid off the saddle and grabbed Star's halter. Quickly, she turned him back to a clump of trees.

Star stepped on a branch. Loudly, it cracked.

"Who's out there?" the man called.

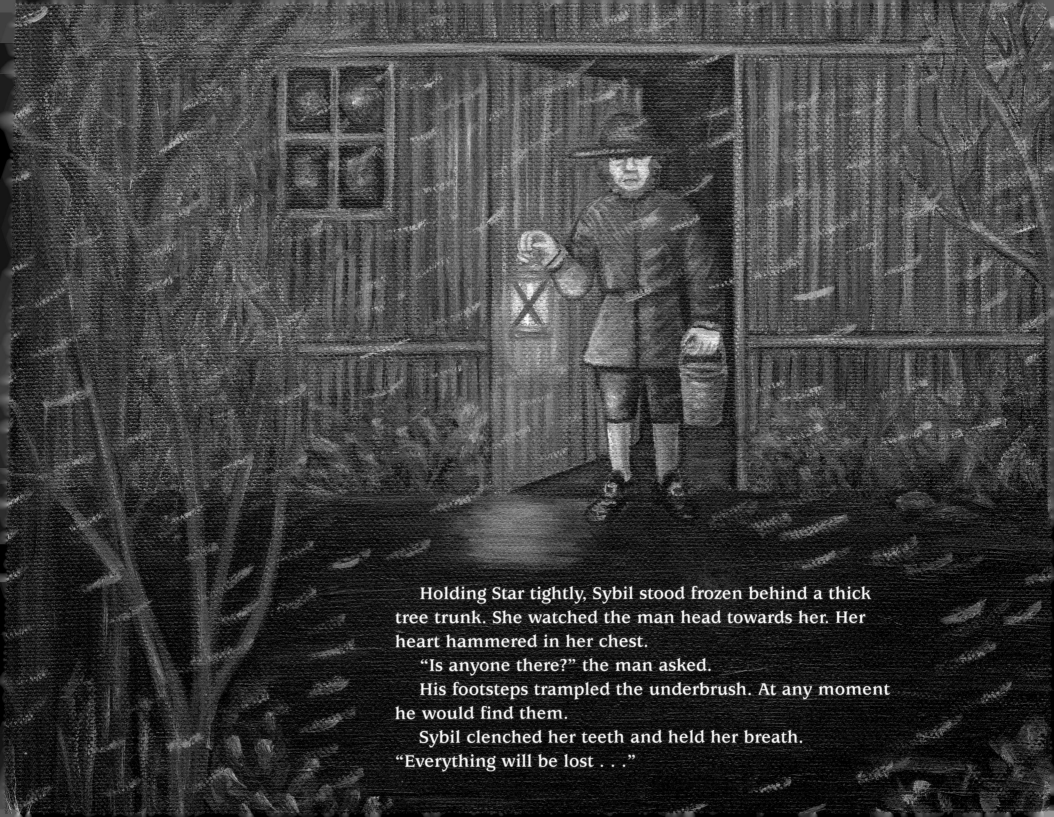

Holding Star tightly, Sybil stood frozen behind a thick tree trunk. She watched the man head towards her. Her heart hammered in her chest.

"Is anyone there?" the man asked.

His footsteps trampled the underbrush. At any moment he would find them.

Sybil clenched her teeth and held her breath.
"Everything will be lost . . ."

"*Whoo-oo*," an owl hooted. "*Whoo-oo*."
The man stopped. "Just an old owl." He turned and went back inside the barn, closing the door behind him.

Sybil hung herself up on the saddle. "Hurry," she urged. Star began to trot. "Faster, boy."

Sybil rode on. All through the night, she gave her alarm: "Muster at Ludington's! Turn back the Redcoats!" Her voice grew hoarse.

Light was slowly spreading through the sky as Sybil turned
away from the last farmhouse. The rain softened to a drizzle.
Sybil hunched over Star as he slackened his pace. Her body
ached. They started for home.

It was a long way back.

At last, she reached the Ludington farm. Sybil pulled Star to a halt. Groups of men were forming ranks. Father stood in the middle of the field, shouting orders. He turned. "Sybil!"

He hurried over and helped her dismount. Then he gave her a long hug.

The men cheered, "Hooray for Sybil!"

Sybil rubbed Star's neck. "We did it, Star. We did it."

Sybil Ludington made her ride on April 26, 1777, through what is now central Putnam County, New York. Sometime later, it was reported that General George Washington visited her home to praise her brave deed.

Fish Kill Village

Brinkerhofs Robelt

Brinkerhofs Bridge

Fish Kill River

Williams ...

bridge

Fish Hill

Jo. Woods

John Wal...

Clove Hill

Bar. ouch
with Barrack

Jacob Woods

Dan Wrights

De Rey's

Bridge

Onah Rush Hill

Bull Hill

Marst Brook

Indian Br.

Hazells Bridge

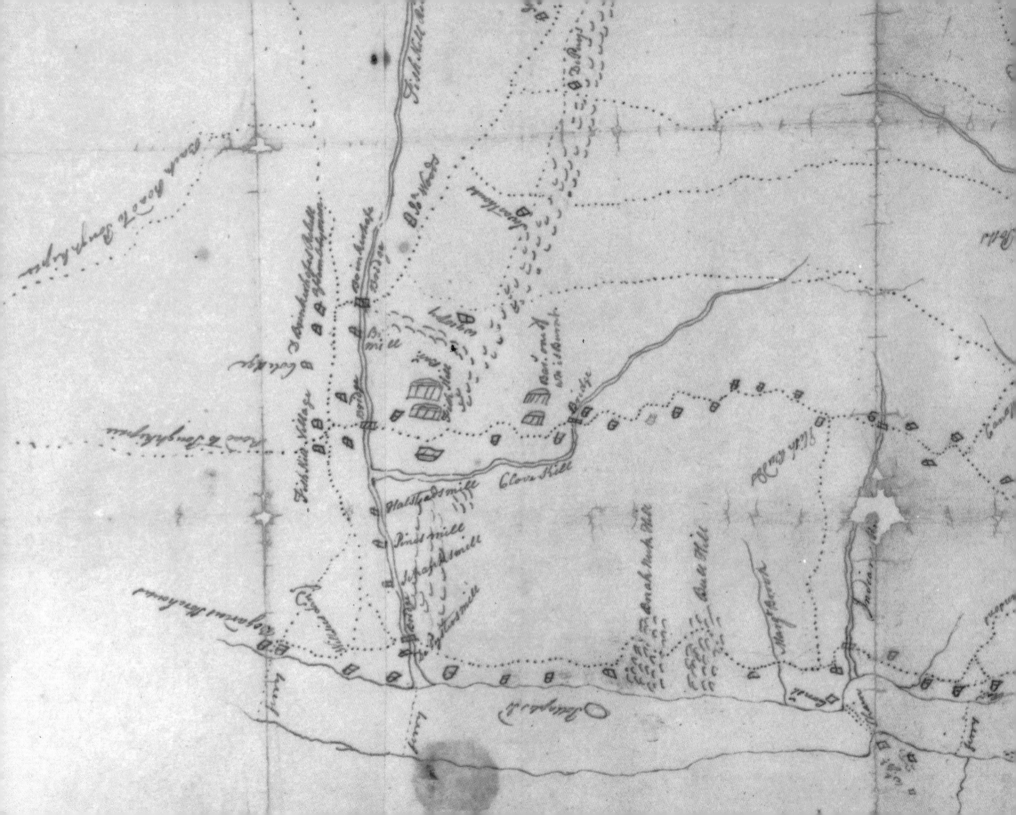